Dear Parent:
Your child's love of reading starts here!

Every child learns to read in a different way and at his or her own speed. Some go back and forth between reading levels and read favorite books again and again. Others read through each level in order. You can help your young reader improve and become more confident by encouraging his or her own interests and abilities. From books your child reads with you to the first books he or she reads alone, there are I Can Read Books for every stage of reading:

SHARED READING
Basic language, word repetition, and whimsical illustrations, ideal for sharing with your emergent reader

BEGINNING READING
Short sentences, familiar words, and simple concepts for children eager to read on their own

READING WITH HELP
Engaging stories, longer sentences, and language play for developing readers

READING ALONE
Complex plots, challenging vocabulary, and high-interest topics for the independent reader

ADVANCED READING
Short paragraphs, chapters, and exciting themes for the perfect bridge to chapter books

I Can Read Books have introduced children to the joy of reading since 1957. Featuring award-winning authors and illustrators and a fabulous cast of beloved characters, I Can Read Books set the standard for beginning readers.

A lifetime of discovery begins with the magical words "I Can Read!"

Visit www.icanread.com for information
on enriching your child's reading experience.

For Anne Hoppe, a great teacher
—L.M.S.

For Ruthie and Dennis
—S.K.H.

HarperCollins®, ☂®, and I Can Read Book® are trademarks of HarperCollins Publishers.

Library of Congress catalog card number: 2006030430
ISBN 978-0-06-054665-6 (trade bdg.) — ISBN 978-0-06-054666-3 (lib. bdg.) — ISBN 978-0-06-054667-0 (pbk.)

12 13 14 15 LP/WOR 20 19 18 17 16 15 14   ❖   First Edition

Follow Me, Mittens

story by **Lola M. Schaefer**

pictures by **Susan Kathleen Hartung**

HarperCollins*Publishers*

"Mittens," calls Nick.

"Let's go for a walk."

Meow! Meow!

"Follow me," says Nick.

Mittens follows Nick.

He follows Nick past trees.

He follows him over logs.

He follows Nick

into the flowers.

Mittens stops.

He smells a flower.

Flutter! Flutter!
A yellow butterfly
flies past Mittens.

It flies up, down,
and all around.

Flutter! Flutter!

Mittens follows the butterfly.

9

Flutter! Flutter!
The butterfly flies
around the bushes.
Mittens follows the butterfly.

Flutter! Flutter!

The butterfly flies over a rock.

Mittens follows the butterfly.

Flutter! Flutter!
The butterfly flies up, up,
and away.

12

Mittens cannot follow
the butterfly.

Mittens stops.

He looks all around.

Mittens cannot see Nick.

Mittens runs over the rock.

He runs around the bushes.

Mittens still cannot see Nick.

Meow! Meow!

"Mittens!" calls Nick.

Mittens hears Nick
call his name.

Mittens follows
the sound of Nick's voice.
Mittens runs and runs.

"MITTENS!"

MEOW!

Mittens sees Nick.

Mittens runs and jumps
into Nick's arms.

PURRRR! PURRRR!

"Follow me," says Nick.

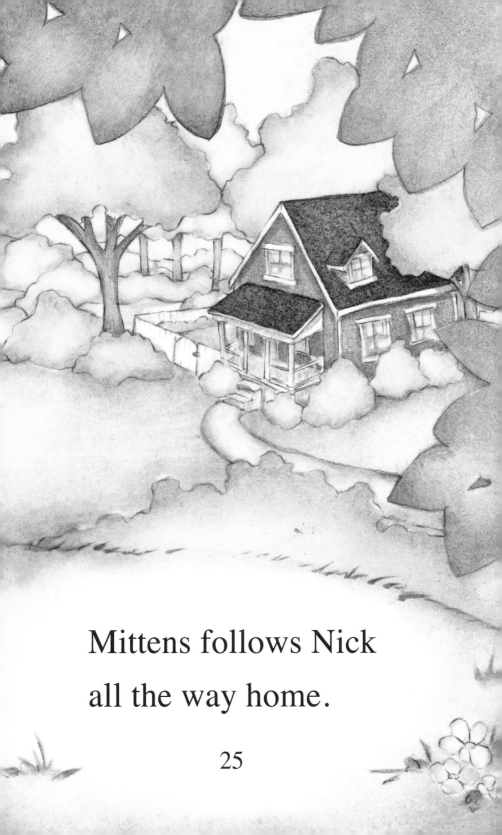

Mittens follows Nick
all the way home.